The Alphabet Book A~Z
SCARECROWS in the GARDEN

By Bobbi Dooley Hunter

HOW TO BUILD A SCARECROW!

It's so easy! Just find a few things around the house, boards, nails, old clothes, a sack, straw, shoes, and garden gloves.

A. Nail 2 boards together like a cross.

B. Put old clothes on your cross, a shirt and pants.

C. Stuff straw inside clothes to fill it out.

D. Put a sack on top and stuff it.

E. Paint a face and top it with a hat.

F. Find your gloves for hands and add shoes for feet.

DONE!

Look for **SQUIRE** the **SQUIRREL** on every page. He sometimes has a pal nearby.

Scarecrows in the Garden © 2022 by Bobbi Dooley Hunter

Written and Illustrated by Bobbi Dooley Hunter

ISBN: 979-8-9857568-3-8

Published by Bobbi Dooley Hunter
Santa Ynez, California

Light of the Moon, Inc.
Partnering with self-published authors since 2009
Book Design/Production/Consulting
Carbondale, Colorado • www.lightofthemooninc.com

THIS IS ONLY THE BEGINNING OF MANY AWESOME ... VEGETABLES!

ART HOKES, the old scarecrow, gets mad if sparrows come to harvest his seedlings. These **ARTICHOKES** take two years to mature but what fun they are to eat.

Rancher Weets does not need much space planting his fast growing **BEETS**! They like cool weather and the leaves and roots are so tasty.

SLOPPY ROTS peers down on this strong crop of **CARROTS**. They will keep producing in cool or warm, but not hot weather. 'Watch out Mr. Rots, everyone likes carrots'!

 **LANKY JILL** has outstretched arms for her lacy **DILL** crop with its yellow flowers. Dill is an herb seasoning for veggies and meats all year.

LEGS SLANT is at peace knowing his summer **EGGPLANT** is healthy and bushy, producing large round, shiny deep purple vegetables that are unique to bake for the family.

OLD MAN JIGGERY

Has no problem
growing hardy
FIG TREES.
The orchard does
well in Spring
and Summer.
Just pick the FIGS
and eat them
right off the TREE!

CEDRICK finds his GARLIC to be so strong that he covers his nose with a handkerchief. This mild~winter crop has bulbs with cloves near the roots. It's so healthy and yummy!

HUCKLEBERRIES grow like shrubs in sunshine under **HARVEY PERRYS'** watchful eyes. These berries are medicinal and delicious fresh off the bush or made into jam and jelly.

Mr. AVERY has tears worrying about his endangered rain forest and the tropical **IVORY NUT PALM** found there. This **PALM TREE** can produce nuts for one hundred years!

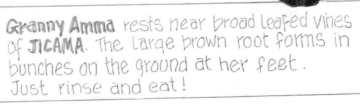

Granny Amma rests near broad leafed vines of **JICAMA**. The large brown root forms in bunches on the ground at her feet. Just rinse and eat!

SISTER GAIL sits patiently while her spring planted crop of **KALE** grows under the sun. These krinkled thick leaves are full of vitamins and are so good for you!

 Miss GLADY'S LETTUCE rows grow in mild, winter climates. There are many kinds and colors of this Leafy, tasty vegetable and they brighten all salads!

MR. FOOMS sits on straw that he uses for compost to grow large MUSHROOMS. They grow in the heat and are good to eat but are not veggies at all. They are FUNGI!

Miss Shums sits on her barrel watching her **NASTURTIUMS** flower. They like spring~time and the stems and flowers can be picked and eaten in salads or stir-fried for a side dish for dinner.

ORKA the headless horsewoman rides near a sun~grown bush of OKRA. This plant is also called Gumbo and is used to make soups and stews.

MISS BUMPKIN loves roasted **PUMPKIN** seeds. She harvests her crop mainly for Halloween and Thanksgiving. These big round yellow squash are fun to carve or bake and eat.

QUINSEY hangs near his crop of **QUINOA!** (keenwa~ meaning mother of all grains). It's red, white or black & is boiled to eat for fiber and protein. It's planted in Spring but likes high and low temperatures.

R

MISS GOLDFARB grows broad leaf red and green **RHUBARB**. This plant takes lots of space in the garden and 2 years to produce stems for slicing, cooking and eating in pies and jellies.

ROY DEAN hunches over his **SOYBEAN** crop which grows through the summer. This good vegetable can be eaten in its green pod, shelled, cooked or dried and is high in protein.

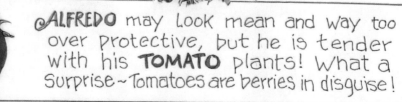

ALFREDO may look mean and way too over protective, but he is tender with his **TOMATO** plants! What a surprise ~ Tomatoes are berries in disguise!

Tinman Chris hovers over his edible crop of **UPLAND CRESS**. It grows like a weed and is good as an herb in salads, adding a fine peppery taste.

DANNY GENE gathers VANILLA BEAN pods from bourbon Orchids in Madagascar or Mexican vanilla plants. It's hard work turning pods into Liquid for baking delicious desserts.

GWILMA HELEN works out among her big green WATERMELON. The summer crop vines over large areas. It's slow growing but so juicy and refreshing!

ELMÃNO collects **XIMENIA** (HEE·M·AI·N·UH) fruit also known as Tallow Wood, Yellow plum or sea Lemon. It grows on a small Leafy tree in the tropics of Southeast Africa.

CAM doesn't mind the hot summer sun. Her YAM crop needs warmth to grow underground. The plant is a sprawling vine with edible roots mostly of water, sugar and starch.

Italian Farmer **BUCCINI** hangs over the **ZUCCHINI**. His summer squash is best harvested as a young plant and the skin, seeds and centers are edible.

This
is not
the end
. . .
of
vegetables

BOBBI DOOLEY HUNTER

Bobbi spent her first 8 years in Portland Oregon with her parents and 2 older brothers. The Family moved to Scottsdale, Arizona where she learned how to ride a horse through the desert! She graduated from the University of Arizona, majoring in Graphic Design and Art History. She has practiced art on every level: advertising, logo design, auto art, welding, and murals on schools, businesses and homes. She has taught art in classrooms for children 1st through 8th grades and continues to produce children's books. She is a wife, mom and grandmother of 4 girls and one little boy. She was a pilot, scuba diver and is now owner/manager of a cattle & farming ranch. She loves life and paints everything she can get her hands on from paper and canvas to walls, trucks and oil pumpers! But mostly, she likes to educate children through her art using bright colors!

Other Works by Bobbi Dooley Hunter

Bobbi and Ken took a long trip to Australia and found Uluru, a big mountain on a flat red desert. At dusk all colors of glowing balls sparkled on the desert floor in front of Uluru. They were placed there as an outside art exhibit by Bruce Munro from London. It was so spectacular, we asked Mr Munro to come to California and place an exhibit in some oak valleys in Paso Robles. We named it SENSORIO!

The Legend of the African Baobab Tree is a story of a beautiful tree who complained to the great spirit of the wild plains about wanting to be the best and brightest and most handsome of all the African trees. The great spirit became tired of the complaints, and reached down from the sky, yanked the tree out of the ground, and placed it back in upside down! All the animals were alarmed, and so was the huge tree. For after that, the magnificent tree only grew leaves once a year. The other months, the roots seem to bend and grow towards the sky.

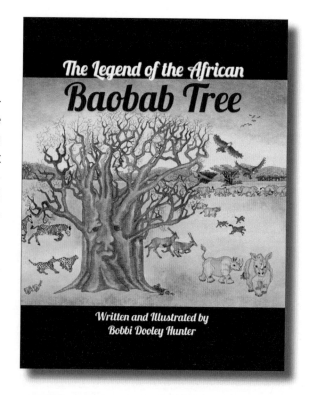

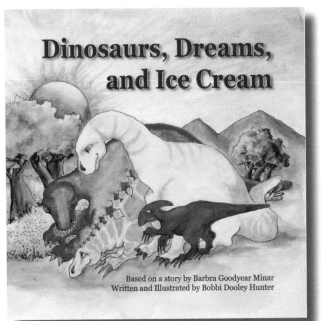

Based on a story by Barbra Goodyear Minar
Written and Illustrated by Bobbi Dooley Hunter

Christopher loves dinosaurs, but they are big and scary. One night, the dinosaurs invited him into their world. Suddenly, he finds himself in a forest, solving a mysterious problem for them. Christopher bravely marches forward, looking for the dinosaurs' stolen ice cream!

This is the story of 'Goldilocks and the Three Bears', but Bobbi shortened sentences by combining phrases, very much like 'Pig Latin'! Languages seem to evolve into short cuts and it's fun to create new words from old phrases. The more you read the story aloud, the easier it is to say and understand! HAVE FUN!

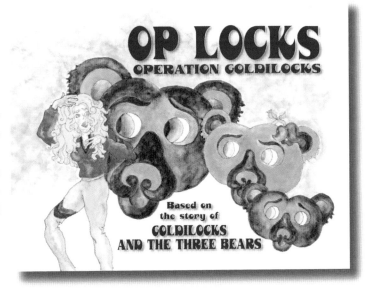

OP LOCKS
OPERATION GOLDILOCKS

Based on the story of
GOLDILOCKS AND THE THREE BEARS

Printed in Great Britain
by Amazon